KISSING
THE DEVIL

KISSING THE DEVIL

John L. Lansdale

BookVoice Publishing

THE MECANA SERIES by John L. Lansdale
#1 - Horse of a Different Color
#2 - When the Night Bird Sings
#3 - Twisted Justice
#4 – The Box

OTHER WORKS BY JOHN L. LANSDALE
-The Last Good Day
-Broken Moon
-Slow Bullet
-Long Walk Home
-Beyond Imagination
-Zombie Gold
-Kissing the Devil
-Shadows West (with Joe R. Lansdale)
-Hell's Bounty (with Joe R. Lansdale)
-Tales from the Crypt (Comic Series)
-That Hellbound Train (Graphic Novel)
-Yours Truly, Jack the Ripper (Graphic Novel)

What Others are Saying about John L. Lansdale

"Mickey Spillane fans will welcome this page-turner...Lansdale effectively delays revealing the novel's big secret until the end. Those who like their thrillers with a heavy dose of violent action will be satisfied." - Publishers Weekly review of Slow Bullet

"This is an entertaining, science fiction-historical-horror blend with resourceful protagonists and a solid cast of secondary characters."
 - Booklist review of Zombie Gold

"Slow Bullet is a straight-ahead thriller...it's about action, and there's plenty of that. Check it out." – author Bill Crider

"...the author's innate ability to spin a complex tale painted with vivid characters and intense suspense provides readers with a well-paced book that they may find difficult to set down...a worthwhile suspenseful ride." - Amazing Stories review of Horse of a Different Color

"Zombie Gold has something for everyone… It's exciting, entertaining and educational. A fun ride." –author Joan Hallmark

"...something unique and comfortable and difficult to put down. Highly recommended." – Cemetery Dance review of Hell's Bounty

"True to Lansdale tradition, John L. Lansdale has compiled a piece of work that should appeal to a wide range of readers."
– Amazing Stories review of Zombie Gold

"Long Walk Home really touched and gripped me. A great bittersweet story of light and shadow about growing up in a time gone by. I loved it." – author Joe R. Lansdale

For certain is death for the born
And certain is birth for the dead;
Therefore over the inevitable
Thou shouldst not grieve.

-- The Bhagavad Gita

PROLOGUE

THE BEGINNING OF FOREVER - THIRTY YEARS AGO

Dancers dressed in ritual costumes moved around a grave on a torch-lit night as the sound of drums boomed out a slow, rhythmic beat.

The top of the grave was stained crimson red from headless, blood-drained chickens. Flower petals were thrown on top of the grave to mix with the blood.

A lone white man and his young son were standing in the midst, staring at the headstone. He stood six-feet-tall with broad shoulders and attention-grabbing green eyes. His eight-year-old soon stood beside him, a smaller mirror image of his father. Both were dressed in hunting clothes, wearing pith helmets and knee-high boots. The man had his rifle sitting in the crook of his right elbow, pointed at the ground.

The dancers continued to chant as they danced around the grave.

A hulking man stood nearby, his body wet with perspiration, his eyes dark. He wore a leopard skin around his waist, different-colored plumage on his head, and a hissing cobra tattoo on his upper left arm. He loosely held a long, crooked stick, pointed toward the grave. A sparkling emerald medallion glowed brightly around his neck.

With lightning quickness, he stretched his arms skyward, holding the crooked stick with both hands at arms length. He pumped the stick up and down, waved it across the grave, and touched it to the emerald. Changing colors burst from the medallion into the night, spilling out over the crowd like a rainbow rain.

The father and son stood awestruck, like toddlers watching fireworks.

The grave began to tremor as dirt slowly separated from the top, uncovering a gold-trimmed casket. The man's arm went limp at the sight and he dropped his rifle to the ground, but made no effort to retrieve it. His son glanced at the fallen rifle, but didn't move.

Suddenly, a crash of thunder shook the ground, and lightning raced across the sky and shot down to the tombstone, shattering it into a thousand pieces. Smoke curled up from the grave. The top of the casket popped open and a human form rose from the grave.

The smoke cleared and a beautiful, cream-skinned woman — very much alive with long, flowing black hair, wearing a white, full-length silk gown — stepped away from the grave and walked toward her husband and son. The crowd separated as she moved closer and closer.

"Joseph, your wife is alive and has returned to you, as we discussed," the hulking man said. "Now it is time you uphold your end of the bargain."

Joseph looked at his son.

"I don't want to go," the boy said and backed away. "Please, don't make me go."

"You have to, Jason. This was the only way to get your mother back," Joseph says. "Go with Samuel, son. He will train you as his apprentice."

The child started to run, but Samuel grabbed him by the hand and dragged him away through the crowd, as Joseph and his resurrected wife could only watch.

I

The iron gates opened and a Rolls Royce drove up a driveway and stopped in front of a mansion that looked like a scene from Gone with the Wind. A well-dressed young man got out and the car drove away.

He went in the mansion and proceeded to a room full of African masks, trophies and a painting of his father. His father's piercing green eyes looked like they were following him as he moved around the room. Two Chinese Pugs ran into the room. He sat down and they jumped up in the chair and licked his face. He grinned and petted them.

A huge man walked in, dressed in a black suit and red tie, with long hair to his shoulders.

"Did you make the arrangements, Jason?"

"Yes, Samuel, don't worry."

"You're the one who needs to worry," Samuel said. "There's no room for any mistakes."

"There won't be. She'll be here in the morning. Her name is Megan Fields."

"Remember, if you can deliver the chosen one, and he accepts her, you will not age and will never die," Samuel said. "Of course, if he doesn't accept her, you will be cast into a burning hell forever."

"Luckily, you have taught me well," Jason said. "I have a plan that can't fail. The master gave me the honor of choosing her. She's a beauty with all the mental and physical qualities needed, and it's the right time to for it. The only thing we have left to do is convert her, willingly or forcibly, to the master's desires. The medallion will take care of that for us."

"Yes it will," Samuel said. "I think you will be joining me in eternal life."

Jason thought about how Samuel appeared to have not aged a day in the thirty years they knew each other.

"Thank you for the confidence," Jason said. "The job is done. I'm going to relax and feed my orchids." He stood up and the pugs jumped off the chair and followed him out of the room.

The next morning, in an apartment building in a suburb of the city, an alarm went off and a young woman sat up in bed. She threw a sheet off her naked body and shut off the alarm. The man beside her rolled over and put a pillow over his head.

"What are you doing up so early?" he asked.

"I have to meet that guy this morning about his antiques. It'll be a great deal," she said. "If we get it."

He sat up. "Of course you will, Megan. But what do you even know about Steinwood? You may not be getting as great a deal as you think."

"He has a lot of valuable antiques that will make me a lot of commission money. That's all I need to know."

She scooted off the bed, slipped into a cotton housecoat, and went to the kitchen.

"You have a flight to Washington at nine this morning. So get your butt out of bed, Gary."

He wiped his blue eyes and got out of bed, stretching his muscular young body. He opened the closet door, took his pilot uniform out and laid it on the bed, then headed to the shower.

After his shower, Gary joined Megan in the kitchen wearing his commercial pilot's uniform with wings on the left side of his coat, a GARY ROBERTS nametag on the right, and a scrambled eggs cap on his head.

"You're going to be late if you don't hurry,"

Megan said, pouring orange juice.

"Why don't you marry me and quit chasing anything but me," Gary said.

"We don't have time to talk about that now," Megan said.

"I'm serious. I've got a three-day flight on the eastern seaboard and when I get back, we get married or I'm leaving. A two-year engagement is too long."

"I'm not ready. This is a new world for me in the city. I need more time to find myself," Megan said.

"Find yourself?" Gary said. "That's stupid."

"Not to me," Megan said.

Megan's black cat Midnight jumped up on the bar, wanting to be fed. Megan opened a can of cat food and sat it in front of him.

"You think more of that damn cat than you do me." Gary stood up. "I'll pick up my things when I get back." He headed for the front door, leaving Megan in the kitchen. She heard the door slam and he was gone.

"Well that was a hell of a surprise," she said to the cat as he gulped down his food. "Looks like we're on our own, Midnight."

She took a shower, put on a chic black dress over her curvy body and red high heel shoes. She brushed her flowing black locks, put makeup on to highlight her beautiful face and brown eyes, and spoke to the mirror.

"I need more time to know if he's the one I want to spend my life with."

She shook her head up and down. The mirror agreed with her.

As she drove to her appointment in her red '65 Mustang convertible, she saw STEINWOOD scrolled in metal over the gate. She pressed a speaker button and a voice came on.

"Yes," the voice said.

"Megan Fields," she said. "I have an appointment with Mr. Steinwood at ten."

"Come in please," the voice said and the gate opened. She drove up a long drive and stopped in front of the mansion. She took a last look in the rearview mirror to check her hair and lipstick and then walked up to the ten-feet-tall double doors and banged the door knocker three times.

The doors opened and a tall man was standing in the doorway with a dog leash wrapped around his wrist. At the other end was a fawn-colored, black-masked Chinese Pug, staring at her.

"Good morning, I'm Megan Fields. I have an appointment with Mr. Steinwood this morning."

"We were expecting you. My name is Samuel. I'm Mr. Steinwood's valet. This is Chester," Samuel said, looking down at the dog. "Come in."

"He's adorable." She bent down and petted him and he licked her hand.

"This way please," Samuel said, leading the dog beside him. They entered a room with a Zebra rug on the floor. A life-sized stuffed lion snarled at her from across the room. Some of the masks on the walls were bright and happy, others dark and grotesque.

Samuel gestured toward a black leather couch for her to sit down.

"Mr. Steinwood will be in shortly," Samuel said. "I must give Chester a bath. Wait here, please."

Megan nodded as Samuel led Chester out of the room, his little legs whirling like bicycle spokes to keep up with Samuel.

Megan looked around the room again and was drawn to the portrait of Joseph hanging over the fireplace. The man in the portrait was dressed in hunter's clothes, his cold, hypnotic green eyes staring at her. She moved closer and a chill ran over her body, drawing her even more into his gaze.

The spell was suddenly broken by a voice behind her. She turned around and smiled.

"Miss Fields, sorry you had to wait," Jason said, holding a different Chinese Pug in his arms.

Jason favored the man in the portrait – good looking with the same green eyes, but younger. He sat the pug on the floor.

"I'm Jason," he said. "Thank you for coming. I see you and father were getting acquainted. Sometimes I think he's going to step out of the painting, it's so real."

"I was thinking the same thing," Megan said.

"He was an avid hunter and worked his diamond mines in Africa. He and my mother were killed in an elephant stampede many years ago on a hunting trip. They never found her body. Have a seat," he said, motioning to a chair.

"I know the sadness," Megan said. "I lost my mother several years ago in a car wreck."

"You do," Jason agreed. "But let's talk about the present. Have a seat please."

Megan sat down in a hand-carved chair, Jason on a black leather couch, and the pug jumped up beside him.

"I contacted Golden House Antiques because they were highly recommended," Jason said. "I want all this sold, you see, and as soon as possible. I have a flight to Africa tomorrow. Samuel will assist you until I return to the US."

"That's fine," Megan said, excited. "I need to do an inventory and prepare a contract."

Jason got up, sat the dog on the floor and walked over to an old roll-up desk.

"My father said this desk once belonged to Benjamin Franklin. Would you like a closer look to evaluate it?"

Megan hesitated for a moment but stood up and walked over to the desk. She knew what he was doing. He knew what it was worth; he wanted to know if she did. The pug was standing by the desk, looking at her.

"Hi Chester," she said.

"You need a closer look, this is Penelope," Jason said. "Samuel has Chester."

"They look so much alike," Megan said and smiled.

"Only at first glance," Jason said and smiled back.

"Sorry, Penelope." Megan grasped the handle and

pulled up. It wouldn't budge. "Looks like its jammed," she said.

"Pull harder, it's not locked," Jason said.

She tugged again and the top flew open, spilling notebooks, papers, coins and jewelry all over the floor. Penelope barked and ran to Jason.

"What have I done," she said and squatted down, picking up the items. "How clumsy of me."

She noticed a sparkling medallion with shining green emeralds, pushed a notebook out of the way and picked it up. The silver-linked chain fell through her fingers. She wrapped her hand around the medallion and squeezed. It moved in her hand like it was alive. She opened her hand and it fell to the floor.

"You like it?" Jason asked.

"It's beautiful," Megan said. The emeralds in the medallion were glowing.

"It would be, if you were wearing it," Jason said. "Would you like to have it?"

"I couldn't afford it," Megan said.

"I'll give it to you," he said.

"Oh no, we can't take gifts from clients," she said.

"Officially, I'm not a client yet. I haven't signed anything." Jason reached down, picked up the medallion, unclasped it and motioned for Megan to turn around.

"No, I can't," she said.

"I insist. My father would have wanted it to be worn by a beautiful woman." He stepped around behind her and placed the medallion on her neck and pushed the clasp closed. It dropped between her breasts. "There, that's where it belongs."

Megan clutched the medallion. She knew she shouldn't take it but something about it excited her, like a lover that she wanted fiercely and shamelessly, knowing she shouldn't.

"Thank you, Jason. I love it," she said.

"Then it's yours," he said. Penelope was sitting at Jason's feet, looking at Megan. Jason smiled, raised Megan's hand to his lips, and kissed her hand.

Megan blushed and dropped her hand. She was fondling the medallion with the other hand without even realizing it.

"Miss Fields, I have to go to my diamond mines tomorrow. Samuel will assist you while I'm gone if you need him. When I come back I will show you the botanical garden where I grow my prize-winning African Orchids."

"I look forward to seeing them. I will cherish the medallion."

Jason rang a bell and Samuel reappeared, leading Chester. He reached down, un-clasped the leash on Chester, and both dogs followed Jason out of the room.

"Samuel, I'll return tomorrow and start the inventory, if that's alright," she said.

"That's fine. Is nine A.M. a good time?" he asked.

"Yes, thank you," she said and they walked to the front doors.

II

The elevator doors opened and Megan made her way down the hall to Golden House Antiques. She opened the door, went in and walked past several empty computer desks of employees at lunch and sat down at her desk. She took a look out a large window at tall buildings across the street and then to an open office door. DAVID BAINES - PRESIDENT was printed on the glass panel of the door; the one next to his was his son's, painted on it was BRAD BAINES - VICE PRESIDENT.

David—in his late fifties, clean-shaven, a little pudgy and wearing a dark blue suit with a red tie over his white shirt—looked up from behind his desk and saw Megan. He stood up, adjusted his suspenders, and walked out to her desk. "You got it," he said.

"How did you know I was going to surprise you?"

David tugged up his pants. "Jason called me and said you had been there and he was very impressed with you. I knew he would. I recommended you, after all. The deal's done thanks to you."

"I still have to do the inventory," Megan said.

"Just a formality, my dear," David said.

"You didn't see it. He has a mansion full of antiques from Africa." Megan rubbed her hand across her breast, touching the medallion under her blouse. She reached for the medallion again, thought better of it and dropped her hand. She knew she should tell David about the medallion but she didn't.

"You're going to get a hell of a commission on this one. Your old man called, just wanted to know how you were doing. I told him you were the best rep I had. I may even have to give you a bonus for this one."

"He's not easy to impress," Megan said. "He didn't want me to leave home."

"He's just a dad worrying about his little girl. You'll always be that to him," David said.

"I guess so," she said. "I thought me and Gary would celebrate, but we broke up this morning. He wants to get married and I don't."

"I'm glad. I never really liked him. He's too bossy for you," David said.

"That was the problem," Megan said.

"How about I throw a party for you and invite your dad," David said. "I'll pay his air fare."

"He probably wouldn't come."

"I'll twist his arm."

"No thanks, I've got enough trouble with him now," Megan said.

A young man wearing a pin-striped blue suit and red tie walked in the front door, carrying a briefcase and interrupted Megan's thoughts. You could tell he was David's son. Taller, but favored his dad with brown eyes, black wavy hair and a neat trim appearance.

He saw his dad and Megan smiling. "What's going on?" he asked.

"Megan closed the Steinwood sale," David said.

"Well congratulations." Brad moved over to Megan and wrapped his arms around her, squeezing her breast against his chest.

Megan pushed away. "I won't have it if I don't get the contract and inventory done," she said.

"By all means, don't let us interfere. Come on, Brad, let Megan do her job."

Megan walked over to the water cooler, Brad watching her hips sway back and forth like a hawk zeroing in on a field mouse. He couldn't take his eyes off her figure.

David noticed him staring. "Can I see you in the office, Brad?"

Brad nodded and followed David into his office. David closed the door behind them.

"Are you stupid," David said. "How many times have you been told to leave Megan alone?"

"I'm just looking," Brad said. "Besides, what about that damn boyfriend of hers?"

"He left on his own this morning. We don't have to worry about him anymore. You're going to get us killed if you don't leave her alone. You know it's hands-off. There are bigger plans for her, and you're not a part of them."

Brad grinned. "Whatever you say, Pop, but sooner or later I'm going to fuck her."

"They already know that's what you're trying to do," David said, "and they're not going to put up with it anymore. Now get out of the office and don't come back as long as Megan's here."

Brad walked behind Megan's chair, leaned over and looked at her breasts from behind and made a kissing gesture, picked up his briefcase and left the office.

Later, Megan looked at the wall clock and gasped. "Oh my, I forgot Carol," she said out loud. She retrieved her phone from her purse and dialed her friend's number.

"You forgot our lunch date," Carol said. "I'm already on my second margarita."

"I'm sorry, Carol, I was at the Steinwoods."

"You get it?"

"Yeah. Got something to show you, too."

"If I'm not drunk by the time you get here."

"I'm on my way."

Megan walked into the restaurant and spotted Carol sitting at a small table for two with three empty cocktail glasses.

"Looks like I got here just in time," Megan said as she walked up to the table.

"Maybe." Carol's coat was draped across the back of her chair. She was a match for Megan's beauty, with blonde hair and big blue eyes.

"I wouldn't wait for anyone else this long, schnuckums," Carol said.

"That's an excuse to get drunk."

"No it's not," Carol said. "You're my best friend. We grew up together in the same backwoods town. Are you hungry?"

"Not really," Megan said. "I'm too excited about the Steinwood deal."

"Food here's not too good, anyway."

"Then why did you want to come here?"

"Convenience? I work across the street."

A young lady with a nose ring, several earrings, and tattoos covering her arms came over to the table with a notepad in her tattooed hand.

Carol looked up at her. "Well, I've definitely lost my appetite now."

Megan gave Carol a nasty look and shook her head no. "Bring us two salads with ranch dressing and coffee."

"I thought you weren't hungry," Carol said as the young waitress walked away.

"We have to order something."

"Why? I've been ordering drinks."

"Never mind, just drink the coffee."

"I'm not drunk," Carol said.

"Okay, you don't have to."

"How did your big deal with Steinwood turn out?"

"Terrific." Megan reached inside her blouse and pulled the medallion out.

"What's that?" Carol asked.

"After I got the deal, Jason Steinwood gave me this. I shouldn't have taken it, but I've never seen anything like it before."

"Did you have to fuck him?"

"Lower your voice, you're drunk," Megan said.

"No I'm not. There's something weird about it, look, the emeralds are pulsating like a heart beating."

"That's silly."

The server returned with the salads and coffee and placed them on the table.

Carol looked down at the food and frowned. "I've got to quit coming here. Looks like something your cat wouldn't eat."

"It doesn't look very good," Megan agreed.

"Well, I've got to go to work. Got a deal myself. Going to sell the Frazier Building."

"You're going to make more money on that than I am off the Steinwood deal."

Carol stood up and leaned to one side a little too much as she removed her coat from the chair. "I might have to do things you wouldn't do," she said. "You can pay for that." She motioned toward the food. "If you want to know more about that thing hanging around your neck, there's an anthropology professor at the university who can probably tell you. Named Beecham. I was in one of his classes for a semester back in the day."

"You don't like it do you?" Megan said.

"Something about it bothers me, don't know what. Got to go. I'll call you later," Carol said with a slur and walked away.

Megan looked at the food, frowned, got up and paid the check and headed back to the office.

Later that evening, Megan was typing out a contract to give Jason when she stopped and looked at the wall clock: 7:30 P.M. She was the only one in the office. She picked up her phone and dialed her dad. After several rings he answered the phone.

"Hello," he said.

"Hi Dad, how are you doing?"

"Hi baby. I'd be better if you were here. With you gone and your mother dead it gets awful lonesome. Tried to call you but you never answer that damn cell phone."

"Sorry, I'll watch for your calls," she said.

"You know, you could get a job here..." As he began speaking, he took off his horn-rimmed glasses and leaned against the wall, brushing his hand through his gray hair then loosening his tie as he sat in his chair next to a table with a picture of him and his late wife Pauline, who was killed in a car wreck five years ago, leaving Jim with an empty home and a broken left leg that has never been the same. Beside their picture was a photo of Megan in her university cheerleader uniform.

"You know, you could get a job here at the university with me, and then we wouldn't have any phone problems."

"I'm just not ready for small-town life, again, Dad."

"That sounds like Carol talking. I blame her for you leaving."

"It has nothing to do with Carol. It's what I wanted to do."

"Where's that flyboy of yours?"

"We're finished. He wants to get married and I'm not ready for that, either."

"That's the only thing you've done right since you left," he said.

"Well I just called to tell you I will be making over a hundred thousand dollars on a sale I just made."

"Doesn't matter. You should come home. Let me know when you come to your senses. I've got to go," he said and hung up.

Megan sat there looking at the phone. "Bye Dad, I knew you would be thrilled," she said to no one. A slow-traveling tear trickled down her cheek. She wiped it away and started looking for her shoes under her desk.

Suddenly, she felt a hand on her shoulder. She jumped, quickly stood up and turned around. Brad was standing there with a big smile.

"Sorry, didn't mean to scare you," he said.

"You scared the hell out of me! You did that on purpose."

"No I didn't, I'm sorry," he said.

Megan slipped her shoes on and cut the computer off. She picked up her purse and headed for the door. "You can lock up, Brad, I'm going home."

Brad moved in front of her. "Why don't we go have a drink and let me apologize."

"Some other time. I have to go," she said and stepped around him.

He grabbed her collar and tore the blouse off her shoulder, causing her purse to fall out of her hand. She pushed him back, reached down and picked up the purse and ran for the door. She opened it and jumped back. Gary Roberts was standing there blocking the door.

"Gary? What are you doing here?" she said, surprised.

Brad stopped in his tracks.

"Thought I would come by and see if you changed your mind. The doorman said you were still here. What happened to your blouse?" Gary motioned to Brad. "Did he do it?"

Brad picked up his briefcase and headed for the door, but Gary pushed him back.

"You do that, asshole?" Gary said, pointing at Megan.

"Get out of my way, flyboy," Brad said.

Gary grabbed Brad and whirled him around and punched him hard in the stomach. Brad wobbled to his knees and dropped his briefcase.

"You touch Megan again, I'll beat your ass like a drum!" Gary yelled.

"Let him go, Gary, I can take care of myself."

"It don't look like it," Gary said.

Brad pushed past Gary, leaving his briefcase on the floor and ran to the elevator. He pushed the call button and looked back at Gary in the doorway. "I'll get you, you sonofabitch," he said. The elevator door opened and he stepped in.

"I told you to leave him alone," Megan said. "You probably just cost me my job and a lot of money."

"If you have to put up with that shit you should have already quit," Gary said.

"My dad made me do everything he said all my life. I could never make my own decisions. Nobody's going to tell me what to do anymore. Including you."

"This was a mistake," Gary said. "You got a head problem I can't help with. I'm outta here." He turned and walked out the door.

Megan slammed the door, sat down on a nearby chair and stared out the window, weeping and wiping away tears. She got up, locked the office door and went home.

III

Megan unlocked the door to her apartment. Midnight came running to her, wrapped his tail around her leg and followed her to the kitchen. She took a can of cat food from the cabinet, turned on the electric can opener and Midnight jumped up on the bar, waiting. She set the bowl of cat food on the floor and he jumped down and gobbled it up.

She kicked off her shoes and peeled her clothes off as she headed to the bathroom. By the time she was there, the only thing she had on were her panties and the medallion. She turned on the water in the shower, checked the temperature until she was satisfied, pulled her panties off but left the medallion on, and stepped into the shower. Little water falls arched from her nipples and splashed rainbows in the tub. Tiny bubbles formed in the silver links of the medallion chain as warm, soapy water rushed down her body and fell in the tub drain. She closed her eyes and felt gentle hands caressing her breasts and moving over her body.

Midnight came to the open door, snarled, and bolted away in a flash.

Megan opened her eyes and the hands were gone. She lifted the medallion and looked at it. The emeralds were shining, pulsating, bright. She cut the water off, grabbed a towel from the rack, wrapped it around her and hurried to the bedroom. She opened the closet and looked around the room. All of Gary's things were gone.

She pulled the silver chain of the medallion up over her head and dropped it on the bed. Midnight jumped up on the bed and, with one quick motion, pounced onto the medallion. He let out a hellish growl. His fur stood up like porcupine quills. He shook the medallion from his paws.

Megan reached for the medallion and Midnight dug four deep furrows in her wrist, spun around, jumped off the bed and ran from the bedroom. A blast of pain shot through her. She pressed the towel against her wrist to stop the blood. The medallion began to glow. She picked it up and dropped the chain around her neck. Suddenly, the cuts on her wrist began to disappear and the pain was entirely gone.

She heard Midnight scratching on the closed balcony door followed by a blood-curling roar. She heard the sound of wind, ran out of the bedroom to the balcony doors. They were wide open and Midnight was sitting on the railing in the falling snow, looking down. He jumped from the second story balcony and landed in the bushes around the building.

She grabbed a coat out of the living room closet, pulled it tight around her, slipped on her boots, opened the front door and ran down the stairs to the bushes, calling for Midnight. No sign of him or any tracks of anything in the snow-covered parking lot. She tried to look in the bushes but the snow blanketed them.

Megan retreated back to her apartment, kicked off her boots and sat down on the couch, placed her head in her hands and slowly slid down on the couch and closed her eyes, mumbling something inaudible about the cat. Within minutes she was lost in a dream, floating on a cloud across a field, African masks like the ones at the Steinwood mansion racing by her, spinning, tumbling, circling her, pressing close with their wooden lips, moving with no words. Her closed eyelids were moving rapidly, the dreams happening at sonic speed. Midnight's face flashed by. An embryo appeared floating over head, growing and changing until a complete baby was formed. The umbilical cord ran from the baby to her. A green lightning bolt darted to the cord and sliced into it like a switchblade knife. The baby drifted away and the cord attached to her disappeared.

A man's face came out of the darkness, coming closer and closer. Smoky air swirled until a fully-developed, golden-tanned man with black shiny hair and sparkling brown eyes was standing naked over her. He bent down and gave her a lingering kiss on the lips. A flash of light from the medallion hit him and he disintegrated as quickly as he appeared.

A scream that wouldn't come out before blasted the sound barrier. Her eyes opened, she was on the couch. She sat up. Her hair was matted across her face from sweat. She brushed her hair back and looked around the room, wild-eyed. No one was there. She grabbed the medallion with both hands, jerked the chain from around her neck and threw it against the wall. A pain hit her in the gut like a hard punch.

There was a banging on her door and then a man's voice. "You alright in there? I heard you screaming."

"Who's there?" she asked, holding her hand on her stomach.

"It's your neighbor, Tom, from across the hall. You need any help?"

Megan put her coat on, went to the door and unlocked it with the night latch still hooked and cracked the door open.

"You remember me," he said, peeking in. "We met at a party down the hall a few months ago."

"I remember you, Tom."

"If you need me just call."

"Thanks, I'll do that." She closed and locked the door.

The stomach pain was getting worse. The emeralds in the medallion were glowing. She picked it up and put it on again and the pain began to go away. She walked naked into the bathroom, with the medallion nestled on her breasts, to wash up. The man she saw in her dream appeared in the mirror, smiling. She jumped back, whirled around to look behind her, but no one was there.

She ran to the kitchen, pulled a drawer open, picked up the biggest knife and sat down against the kitchen wall with the knife in her hand. She saw her phone on the kitchen table. She couldn't remember Tom's number. She looked at a clock on the kitchen bar: 2:16 A.M. A strong wind rattled the glass balcony doors. She could see snow sticking to the doors for a moment before sliding down into a pile. No sign of Midnight.

She reached up on the bar, pulled the phone off and sat back down against the wall, clutching the knife in one hand and the phone in the other.

She dialed Carol but the phone only rang and rang with no answer. She slowly got to her feet and held the butcher knife, ready for action. She moved toward the bathroom. She peeked at the mirror and saw herself. She waited for someone else to appear but they never did.

Her phone rang and she jumped. It was Carol.

"Sorry I called you," Megan said.

"No problem."

"I was having bad dreams and then Midnight jumped off the balcony."

"Hope he's got some of his nine lives left," Carol said. "You need me?"

"I'm alright now," Megan said. "Did I wake you?"

"No, I was taking care of business."

"At two in the morning?"

"You don't need to know," Carol said. "What kind of bad dreams were you having?"

"Midnight got tangled up with the medallion and went bonkers and jumped off the balcony and then I started having horrible dreams about a naked man."

"That don't sound all bad, but the medallion may be cursed," Carol said. "That's probably why you're having those dreams."

"Do you know Jason?" Megan asked.

"Seen him at several parties, he was always trying to get in my pants. Never been married, I've been told. He's too involved with those diamond mines his daddy left him. Extremely rich and eccentric. You should go talk to that professor about the medallion."

"I'll call him tomorrow," Megan said.

"Good, let me know what he says. Got to go, bye."

Megan cut her phone off and walked back to the bathroom and looked in the mirror again. No one there but her. She started to take another shower but thought better of it and went to the bedroom, laid down on the bed with the butcher knife and phone next to her hand and pulled a sheet over her.

Across town in the wee hours, a lone shadowy figure was hiding behind the trunk of a big oak tree across the street from Brad Baines' house. The lights in a bedroom were on, showing silhouetted figures of a man and a woman behind drapes, moving back and forth across a large second-story window. The lights went out and the figures disappeared.

Moonlight crept through the window, spreading a soft dim glow across the room. Brad was standing at the foot of the bed in his underwear. He grabbed a sheet on the bed covering a pretty naked woman and pulled on it. She grabbed and flipped the sheet down to show her large breasts and covered them again with the sheet, laughing. Brad crawled up on the bed under the sheet toward her.

Across the street, the shadowy figure lifted a crooked stick up in the air and pointed it toward Brad's house. The knob on the front door turned and the door opened. Two big gray wolves appeared out of nowhere and walked across the lawn into the house. They stopped in the foyer, looked up the stairs and started climbing the steps.

As the wolves approached the bedroom door, the door knob turned and the door cracked open. Brad and the woman were under the sheet, laughing and rolling around on the bed. The wolves began to growl. Brad and the woman heard the sound and threw off the sheet. The wolves, growling, showed their big white teeth. The woman screamed and pulled the sheet up over her body like it would protect her.

Brad jumped from the bed and one of the wolves leapt on him in mid-air and brought him down beside the bed. Brad screamed. The sound of growls and grinding teeth filled the room. Brad rose up from the side of the bed, one of his hands missing, blood shooting out of his arm. The wolf pulled him back down to the floor.

The woman on the bed was screaming hysterically, watching the wolf tear Brad apart. The other wolf was watching and waiting for her to move. She threw the sheet off and crawled to the end of the bed as fast as she could, jumped off the bed and ran toward the door. The wolf ran to her and jumped on her back. She staggered out the door and into the hall, the wolf on her back, sinking his teeth into her neck, blood shooting out in all directions. She fell and tumbled down the stairs, knocking the wolf off, then began crawling towards the front door. The wolf caught up, grabbed her arm, spun her around and chewed it off. She scooted face-down a few feet on the slippery blood-soaked floor, then stopped moving, as blood pooled around her.

The wolf picked up an arm with a big diamond ring on the hand. The other wolf joined him, blood dripping from his mouth. They walked out the door, the wolf carrying the woman's arm and dropped it on the lawn.

They stood perfectly still on the lawn, watching the hidden figure wave the stick in the air and the wolves disappeared. The only thing left on the lawn was the woman's arm lying in the plush green grass, the diamond ring sparkling on the hand in the moonlight.

Lights came on in some of the houses on the street. The shadowy figure and the wolves were gone.

IV

A little after seven the next morning, Megan woke up and looked around the room, picked up her phone and butcher knife, and made her way to the kitchen. She sat the phone and knife on the counter and washed her face in the sink. After pouring a glass of orange juice, she went to the living room and sat down in front of the TV.

David Baines was on the news. "My son didn't have a face…he was torn to pieces!" David sobbed to a young reporter holding a microphone.

Megan's juice glass tumbled out of her hand and busted into pieces on the floor. She lost her breath for moment and gulped for air.

"We're very sorry for what happened to your son and his friend," the reporter said. David nodded, wiped tears from his eyes and walked away.

The camera turned back to the reporter. "This is Jan Abbot, reporting live from the Baines residence." A reporter from the studio came on air with the next story.

Megan's phone rang.

"Did you see the news?" Carol asked.

"Caught the end of it. What happened?"

"Brad and one of his girlfriends were horribly murdered last night," Carol said. "Something ripped them apart. If they hadn't have been inside Brad's house, the police probably couldn't have identified them."

"I feel so sorry for David," Megan said. "Didn't think much of Brad, but, still, that's a terrible thing to happen to someone."

"I feel the same way," Carol said. "I know you want to do something for David but I don't know what it could be."

"Express our sympathy and go to Brad's funeral is about all we can do."

"I'll go with you."

"I can always count on you," Megan said.

"That's what best friends are for," Carol said. "I'll come over and keep you company."

"I'll come to you. I need a bath."

"Why can't you take one there?"

"I'll tell you when I get to your place. See you

soon."

"Okay, I've got plenty of soap."

Megan turned the TV off and dialed her phone.

"Steinwood residence," Samuel said.

"Hi Samuel, this is Megan Fields. I have to postpone the inventory. Something terrible has happened. Mr. Baines' son was murdered last night and it's going to be several days before I can get back to you."

"I will convey that to Mr. Steinwood," he said. "Pass on our condolences."

"I will, thank you," Megan said and hung up.

Megan's phone rang again. "Hi Dad, I was about to call you. David's son Brad is dead. Someone murdered him and his girlfriend last night."

"I saw it on the news. I called David but he didn't answer the phone. Wasn't sure you would, either."

"Here I am," Megan said.

"Tell David I'll come to the funeral. It'll also give me a chance to see you and try to talk you into coming back home. Your room looks just like it did when you left."

"This is not the time, Dad."

"It never is," he said.

"I'll call you when I know when Brad's funeral is. I have to go meet Carol now."

"Tell her I said hello."

"I will."

"David saved my life in combat…I owe him."

"I know," Megan said.

"I'll let you go. Bye, sweetheart."

"Bye."

She went to her bedroom and opened the closet door, took out hangers with jeans and a red pullover sweater and dropped them on the bed. She started to close the closet door when one of Gary's uniforms caught her eye. She didn't move for several seconds as she stared at the uniform, then closed the closet door, put on her clothes and boots and stuck her keys and phone in her pockets.

She heard the balcony doors rattling again. She walked out of the bedroom toward the sound. Something black was on the railing in the falling snow. Her first thought was Midnight. She hurried to the door and a big raven was sitting on the rail. It turned to look at Megan. It looked like there was fire in its eyes. It spread its wings in the falling snow, screamed bloody murder and flew away.

V

Megan, Jim and Carol walked away from the grave to a waiting limo, the driver holding open the doors. David was getting into another car to go back to an empty home.

Megan looked out the window and Carol and Jim sat like zombies as the limo rolled along toward the airport.

Jim broke the silence. "Megan, I realize I'm the one who called my army buddy to get you a job but it was a mistake. You don't belong here. I have a feeling something bad is going to happen to you."

"Carol is going to take care of me," Megan said.

"Right, Carol?"

"No speak-a the English," Carol joked.

The limo stopped at the boarding entrance to the airport. The driver got out and removed the luggage from the trunk and sat it on the sidewalk. Jim handed the driver a tip and picked up his luggage. Megan and Carol hugged Jim's neck.

"She'll be alright, Mr. Fields. I'll see to it," Carol said.

"Come home, Megan. I need you."

"I have to grow up some time, Dad. I'll come home for a visit after I finish the Steinwood sale."

"You two watch out for each other. Carol, you come with her if she comes home."

"Thanks, I will," Carol said.

Megan hugged his neck again. He picked up his luggage and headed for the entrance, stopped, looked back at them, waved and continued on. Megan and Carol got back in the limo and the driver drove away.

Thirty minutes later, Megan and Carol walked into Megan's apartment, Carol carrying a sack and Megan a large pizza box, and made their way to the kitchen.

"Glad we're done with the funeral," Megan said. "I hate what happened to him, but I have to admit, I'm relieved I don't have to put up with him anymore."

"Yeah, I was freezing my butt off. It didn't stop snowing until the funeral was over. I think that was because he was a jerk," Carol said. "Where's his mother?"

"David and Brad never spoke about her. No one

knows," Megan said.

"Does your dad know?"

"I don't think so. I've never heard him say anything about her."

"Changing the subject," Carol began, "you think your dream man will show up again tonight?"

"I hope not," Megan said.

"If he does, I might have to take over for you."

"You're not funny."

"Everyone's a critic. Where's the corkscrew? I'll open a bottle," Carol said.

"In the drawer in front of you," Megan said. "Thanks for coming over, by the way. I needed some company after dealing with the funeral, and Dad."

"You may be too hard on your dad. He just wants to make sure you're safe. My parents couldn't wait for me to get out. When I turned eighteen they packed my clothes."

"You're exaggerating."

"Not much. I was the last of the bunch and they wanted an empty nest. I don't bother them and they don't bother me."

Megan sat two wine glasses and two plates on the table and put a slice of pizza on each plate.

"I can't find the corkscrew," Carol said. "Am I going to have to open this with my teeth?"

Megan opened the drawer and handed it to Carol.

"Thanks." Carol opened the bottle and poured wine in the glasses, then sat down and took a bite of pizza and a sip of wine. "Want me to call Gary for you?"

"No," Megan said.

"I think you're making a mistake. He loves you. But, it's your life."

"I love him, too, but it's like he wants me to be one of his possessions."

"I don't think that's right, either, but I'm no expert on men. I do know how to enjoy them, though. While you were being a good little girl making A's in college I was partying and fucking my way through the football team."

"You have no shame, do you?" Megan said.

"No," Carol said and they both laughed. Carol noticed the medallion chain around Megan's neck. "When are you going to see the professor about that medallion?"

"I haven't had time yet. I get severe pain when I take it off. But when I put it back on, the pain goes away."

"Jason knew what it would do," she said.

"I don't think so," Megan said. 'There must be a logical explanation."

"Professor Beecham knows more about curses and black magic than anyone else I know. I had two classes with him. It was interesting as hell, but scary. He told us about these devil worshipers who could create spells that would drive a person insane, and much more."

"I don't believe in black magic. Or curses. It has to be something simple, like an allergy, or something else more explainable."

"Go see him. You'll change your mind." Carol

poured more wine. "If Beecham can't help, I'll go kick Jason's ass for giving you that damn thing."

"No, it's my problem. I'll handle it." Megan picked up a slice of pizza and placed it on Carol's plate, then got one for herself. "Let's eat."

"You want some company tonight?" Carol asked.

"If you want, but I'm alright. I had a bad dream, that's all. I'm going to take the medallion back tomorrow."

"Go see the professor before you see Jason."

"I don't think that's necessary," Megan said.

"Yes it is," Carol said. "What's happening to you sounds supernatural."

"That's ridiculous."

"No it's not. Promise me you'll see the professor before going to Jason."

"I have to inventory his stuff. And I haven't talked to David or Samuel about it since Brad was murdered."

"Don't do it before you talk to Beecham. He told us about very strange things he witnessed in villages across Africa, Europe and Asia. Witch doctors and all that."

"And you actually believed them?" Megan asked.

"Yes! He was serious."

"Fine, I'll call him in the morning. Satisfied?"

"Yes. I'll spend the night with you for the hell of it," Carol said.

"You may be disappointed. I don't think my dream man will be back," Megan said.

"You never know." Carol smiled.

Megan and Carol went to bed and had a peaceful night.

Outside, the raven had returned and was walking up and down the balcony railing, looking into the apartment with his fiery eyes. He sat motionless for a few seconds before flying away into the night.

VI

After Carol left the next morning, Megan walked into the bathroom, looked in the mirror and saw her face. "My imagination is going wild." She took a quick shower with the medallion hanging around her neck then called the university to speak with Professor Beecham. He told her to come by after classes—3:30 P.M. in Room 106—and he would take a look at the medallion.

That afternoon, she pulled into the parking lot and walked through some remaining snow, up to the double doors of the building and proceeded down a long hallway. Standing outside Room 106, she looked through a small glass panel on the closed door and saw a roly-poly-looking old man with a gray beard, sitting at a desk and looking at a paper in his hand. There were dozens of chairs in the room, a row of windows with the blinds closed, and a blackboard on the wall behind him.

She walked up to the desk and stopped in front of him. "Are you Professor Beecham?"

Jolted, he dropped the paper on the desk and looked up at her.

"Yes, I'm Professor Beecham. Sorry, I didn't see you come in. You scared the living daylights out of me."

"My name is Megan Fields. I called you earlier about the medallion."

"Oh, yes, I remember. Did you bring it with you?"

"I have it on." She reached inside her blouse and pulled the medallion out, the emeralds sparkling.

"Would you mind handing it to me so I can get a better look?"

"Can't you see it from there?"

He stepped a little closer, pushed his glasses up on his nose and shook his head.

"That's what witch doctors call a chakra. They are often found in the cradle of humanity, Africa, although their true origin remains unknown. It is believed to be associated with evil, a tool of the devil to control the wearer, especially women the devil desires. Legend has it the devil will send an incubus before he comes for you."

"What's an incubus?" Megan asked.

"A fallen angel, deceptive and evil, who has a demonic encounter with you controlled by the devil."

"You're kidding. Surely a man with your education doesn't believe that."

"If you're so sure then take the medallion off," he said. "We'll both have a good laugh."

Megan lifted the chain up over her head and removed the medallion. A severe pain hit her in the gut. She felt as if her skin was being peeled off. She threw the medallion against the wall. It fell to the floor and the emeralds began to glow and pulsate even more brightly.

A grinding sound like a freight train coming to a halt jarred the room, sending a deafening sound bouncing off the walls.

Beecham fell to the floor, holding his hands over his ears.

Megan also covered her ears. Her legs became sticks that wouldn't move. She used all her strength to edge her way toward the door, taking tiny sips of air to suppress nausea. A green mist appeared and filled the room, and turned her face a pale pink.

With a burst of energy, Megan took a big step, grabbed the door handle and saw the bolt on the door slam into the lock.

A chair leg tapped. Then another, and another, until the hammering joined the train sound to form a maddening crescendo.

Beecham was tossing around on the floor with his hands over his ears, perspiring profusely.

Megan turned to the wall, her hands over her ears, the mist curling around her like a snake.

Chair legs popped and pounded on the floor. The legs began to flex like lean muscular jungle cats. The room darkened from the mist covering the fluorescent lights.

The chairs began to move in unison toward Megan. She was pressed against the wall like a picture frame as they closed in on her.

Beecham struggled to his feet, staggered past one of the moving chairs, scooped up the medallion and dropped the chain over Megan's head. It fell around her neck and the mist instantly evaporated. The chairs stood still and the fluorescent lights could be seen again.

Megan's eyes darted around the room in fear.

Beecham wiped his brow with a handkerchief. He sat down in his chair and exhaled.

"I closed the gates of hell. You're safe for now as long as you don't take that medallion off."

Megan stepped away from the wall.

"Where did you even get it?" Beecham asked.

"A man named Jason Steinwood gave it to me. I closed a deal to sell his antiques."

"I know of Jason, and his father. There's a story of how a witch doctor brought Mrs. Steinwood back from the dead many years ago in Africa. It's a mysterious place... I don't know enough to fight the forces of hell myself, but I know a priest who does."

"I don't believe that's the reason Jason gave it to me."

"You saw what happened when you took the chakra off. And that's just the beginning. The only way to fight it is with the help of a man of god. We could call the cops, but they wouldn't believe us, and couldn't do anything to help you, anyway."

"When can we see him?" Megan asked.

"I'll call him. His name is Father Tijeras of San Gabriel Cathedral. He was raised in an African village that was destroyed by a volcano many years ago." He dialed the phone and Father Tijeras answered.

"Father, I have a young lady here who needs your help." Beecham held the phone, explaining the situation and listening. Finally, he said, "Okay, thanks, we'll see you tomorrow," and closed his phone. He turned to Megan. "He said come to San Gabriel's tomorrow evening after mass and he'll help you."

"Why not now?" Megan said.

"He said he has to prepare for a ritual in order to do you any good."

"You believe he can get rid of it?"

"Yes. I'll go with you. You shouldn't go home if you live alone until we see him."

"I do," Megan said.

"You can stay at my place. I'll cancel my classes for tomorrow. You're running out of time before the devil takes control of you."

"Why do you want to help me?" Megan asked.

"I won't if you don't want me to."

"I'll go with you," Megan said. "Should I call the cops on Jason?"

"Not yet. Meet me outside. I'm driving a gray Volvo."

"I'm in a red Mustang," Megan said.

"Let's go."

Twenty minutes later, Beecham and Megan pulled into the driveway of his large brick house with a two car garage. Both garage doors opened and they drove in side by side. Beecham unlocked the kitchen door and they went inside.

"There's a bedroom down the hall on the first right," Beecham said. "I'll lock up. Feel free to lock your door."

Megan walked down the hall, went in the room and sat down on the bed. The room had white walls, flowery pink drapes hanging over two windows, and a pink bedspread to match with a big, white teddy bear on the bed. There was gold trim on white French-style end tables and a chest. A school cheerleader picture of a girl was sitting on an end table. A large portrait of the Eiffel Tower was hanging on the wall. She could see from the open door to the bathroom a row of lights over a mirror and the same styled sink as the furniture.

There was a knock on the door. "Miss Fields, I have some fresh towels for you, if you want them."

Megan opened the door and Beecham was

standing there with an arm full of towels and a net sack of delicate soap. Thought you might need this. I'm across the hall if you need me." He walked in and left the door open.

"Thanks, this is a very pretty room," Megan said.

"It was my daughter's when she was a teenager. Lost her and my wife in an airplane crash several years ago. Just left it like it was."

"Sorry to hear that."

"They were going to France for a visit. My daughter liked the French style and wanted to see Paris. That's why the room is decorated the way it is."

"She had good taste."

"Thanks. You like spaghetti?"

"Yes," Megan said.

"I'm a mean spaghetti chef. I'll add some good garlic bread, too."

"Sounds good to me."

"Alright. Be about an hour and then we can find out more about each other."

"Sounds good," Megan said. Beecham turned back to the open door, walked out and closed it behind him.

Megan dialed Carol but no answer. She called four more times without an answer, even trying her realty company, but they were also having trouble finding her.

After checking with a boyfriend and two more places, she gave up and called David.

"Hi Megan, where are you?" he said.

"I'm so sorry about Brad, David. I called to tell

you Jason gave me a medallion. I didn't tell you about it before and now it's causing me trouble."

"What kind of trouble?" he said.

"I'll tell you later. I'm going to have to take off a few days. I can't go back to the Steinwoods. If you want to fire me I understand."

"I'm not going to fire you. I would be glad to help if I can. Where are you?"

"Thanks, but it's something I have to do myself. I have to go, talk to you later."

There was a tap on the door. Megan got up and opened the door slowly. Beecham smiled at her.

"I'm working on the spaghetti. Why don't you join me, we can talk."

"Okay. I'll just wash up and be right there."

Beecham nodded and headed back to the kitchen.

A few minutes later, Megan joined him and sat down on a bar stool.

"You have anymore relatives here?" she asked.

"No, I came from England in the sixties when I was a teenager. The rest of my family stayed there and have all passed away." He checked the spaghetti and turned back to Megan. "What about you?"

"I was raised in a little town in Texas and then took off for Chicago to get some city excitement. My dad got me a job with Golden House Antiques that an army buddy of his owns. He has regretted it ever since. I think he thought I wouldn't like it and would come home for good, but he was wrong. My dad's a professor there, teaches literature. Keeps hounding me to come home and teach. But I lost my mother in a car wreck there, which was too much of a reminder every day."

"And you think teaching is boring," he said.

"Until now," she said and smiled.

"This is not theory, it's real. It's not to be taken lightly. How did you find out about me?"

"My best friend, Carol West. She was a student of yours some time back."

"That name sounds familiar."

"She said she took two classes with you and was very fond of you."

Beecham rolled his eyes, looking at the ceiling. "I think it's coming to me. A pretty, blonde-headed girl with a mischievous smile?"

"That's her. We grew up together. She works for a realtor now."

"Does she know what's happened to you?"

"Some. Not as much as we do. She knows Jason. I'm afraid she may have went to see him, trying to protect me. She promised my dad she would. She doesn't know how serious this is."

"That medallion you have is meant for a chosen one."

"Chosen for what?"

"To breed with the devil. For a son. If the baby is a female, you and the baby will die before it's born."

"I would kill myself before I would submit to the devil," Megan said. "How did you get involved with this kind of thing?"

"I've always been fascinated with archeology. Father Tijeras and I met years ago on a dig in Africa.

He took me to a village where the local witch doctor was raising people from the dead."

"Are you serious?" Megan asked.

"Absolutely. I saw it. That's how I know what you're up against."

Megan looked at the stove. "The spaghetti is boiling over," she said.

"Oh my!" Beecham grabbed a glove and lifted the pot off the flame. "Almost burned it," he said.

"Looks okay to me."

"I'll finish dinner, you keep trying to get a hold of your friend."

"Sometimes Carol does go off partying and stays out all night. Maybe that's why she's not answering her phone..."

After dinner, Megan went back to the bedroom, locked the door and got on her phone again to find Carol. Still no luck.

The next morning her phone rang, but it was only Carol's work.

"This is Empire Realty. Carol had you listed as her emergency contact. Is she with you?"

"No," Megan said. "I can't find her."

"We went to her residence. The landlord let us in. The bed hadn't been slept in. The landlord said he saw her get in a car with two men yesterday. He didn't know them, and we didn't have her scheduled to see any clients."

"Have you called the police?"

"Not yet," the voice said.

"Did the landlord say what they looked like?"

"Yes. One was a good-looking thirty-something, and the other one was a big, muscled-up black guy wearing an unusual multi-colored shirt."

"I know who they are," Megan said. "I'll call the police. Better yet, I'll go see them. Thanks, I'll let you know when I find her."

Megan knocked on Beecham's bedroom door. "You in there, professor?"

"Yes, I'll be right out."

Megan put yesterday's clothes back on and walked into the kitchen. Beecham joined her by the time she got there.

"Can I fix you breakfast?" he asked.

"No, I'm not hungry. Thanks, though."

"How are you feeling?"

"Okay right now, but Carol may not be. I found out she got in a car with two men yesterday outside her apartment. The description fits Jason and his valet, Samuel, and she didn't come home last night. I have to go to the police. I know you said the priest is the only one who can help me but I have to help Carol. I'm going to have them look for her at Jason's."

"Don't go. Call the cops instead."

"I have to go in person to make sure they actually get someone to look for her."

"You should stay put until we visit the priest," Beecham said. "I hate to tell you this, but the devil worshipers make sacrifices of those close to the chosen ones to appease the devil if they're having trouble delivering the chosen one, and it looks like they are. Of course, there's the possibility they're innocent, but I don't think so. Especially with you wearing the chakra."

"Why did they pick me?"

"No idea," Beecham said. "Where's your former boyfriend?"

"I don't know. I've called him several times, too, but no answer. He's a commercial pilot and takes extra flights sometimes when he wants to get away."

"The devil worshipers may have murdered him. They may even come after me now."

"What a disgusting and chilling thought."

"I'll go with you to the police."

"No, I already have Carol to worry about," Megan said. "I don't want to have to worry about you, too. Wait for me here. I'll be back soon."

"It's really too dangerous for either of us to venture out until we visit the priest."

"I have to do what I have to do."

"At least promise me you won't go to the Steinwood Mansion," Beecham said.

"I promise."

Megan fished the Mustang keys out of her pocket and hurried to the garage and backed out. Beecham waited until she cleared the driveway then got in his car and backed out. He spotted the red Mustang turning at the next street corner and followed, keeping several car lengths between them. When he saw Megan park down the block from the police station, he slowed down and parked where he could see the front of the building with a good view. Two uniformed police officers walked out the door as Megan went in.

He didn't know Jason and Samuel were parked three cars behind him.

Megan looked the place over. The interior was drab. Several desks were jammed up against each other in a long line, papers scattered all over them. No one sat at any of the desks except for a man with a sign that read INFORMATION and a name plaque on his desk that read SERGEANT A.J. WAXMAN. He was in his forties or early fifties with a chubby red face, thin hair, and looked like he had been poured into his uniform. Definitely not a poster boy for recruitment.

He looked up at Megan. "Can I help you, miss?"

"Yes. My best friend has disappeared and I think I might know where she is."

"If you know where she is why don't you go get her?"

"It's complicated," Megan said.

"Well, simplify it for me. How long has she been missing?"

"Since last night."

"Lady, you're wasting my time. I can't file a missing persons report for an overnight disappearance."

"She might have went to confront a client of mine, one who is dangerous and could hurt her."

"A client of yours? You're not a..."

"No! I'm not a prostitute. I work for Golden House Antiques and she works for Empire Realty."

"No judge is going to approve a request when she hasn't even been missing twenty-four hours."

"If I give you the name of the person and address of where she may have gone, can't you at least take a look?"

"Do you see anyone here besides me? We're very busy."

And with perfect timing, a plain-clothes cop walked in. She could see his badge on his belt.

"What about him," she said.

"Sergeant Howard, come here a minute please."

Howard strolled over. "What you need, A.J.?" He was a neat-looking little man with a black mustache to match his tanned face, wearing a dark blue suit with a red tie.

"This lady's got a friend missing, but she hasn't been missing long enough to file a report. She says she's in danger, gave me a name and address of someone she thinks may have kidnapped her. You think you could check it out without a report?"

"Maybe tomorrow," Howard said.

"It has to be now," Megan said. "And you'll need help. Don't go by yourself. He may kill you, too."

"I'll make a stop on the way home. Give me the info."

"Don't go alone," Megan repeated. "Here's my phone number." She wrote it on a notepad and handed it to the officer.

"Go ahead and fill out the form, miss," A.J. said.

Megan filled out the form then walked outside the police station to her Mustang. She noticed a gray Volvo sedan like Beecham's was parked on the block behind her, with no one else around. She hesitated for a moment, looking at the car, started to take a closer look, but changed her mind and headed back to Beecham's place.

She called him on the way. No answer. The setting sun behind tall buildings to the west reminded her it would be time to see the priest soon. She wasn't sure she had the courage to go without the professor. She had to find him. Going back to the police would only add to their confusion and do nothing to help.

When she arrived at Beecham's house, he was nowhere to be found. She wheeled out of his place and headed for Carol's. She called Carol and Beecham again with no luck.

She parked her Mustang outside Carol's apartment building and made her way upstairs. She opened the door with the key Carol gave her and went inside. No sign of Carol. All of her clothes were still in the closets. She walked out of the apartment, locked the door and walked down the hall to the elevator. When it opened, Gary was there wearing jeans and a leather jacket. They both looked surprised to see each other.

"I've been looking everywhere for you," Gary said. "I don't want to lose you. I love you."

"I love you too," Megan said. "Maybe I do have head problems like you said."

"I was just mad. Let's make up and try again."

"I want to, but I have some other problems I have to take care of first."

"Like what?" Gary asked.

"The Steinwood thing has turned into a

nightmare. I have this medallion I can't take off and now I need a priest's help to get rid of it before I get sent to the devil."

"What? If you don't want me just say so," Gary said.

"No, it's true," she said. "I know it's hard to believe, but it's true. I think they have Carol and I'm next."

"I'm going by your place to get my things," Gary said. "I'll leave the key under the doormat. I get the message. Don't worry, I won't be back again." He turned back to the elevator and punched the down button.

"Gary, I'm telling you the truth!"

"Bye Megan." Gary rolled his eyes as the doors closed.

She stood there, watching the arrow on the floor lights drop as the elevator descended. She went downstairs, got back in her Mustang, and debated whether she should go to the Steinwoods to look for Carol, or to the church.

Everything pointed to the medallion as her main problem. She would go to the church first and Gary could go to hell.

VII

Samuel climbed a stairwell to a trap door underneath the life-like stuffed lion in the house. He raised the door, tilting the lion over, got up on the house floor and dropped the door and lion back into place, lion hair falling to the floor.

Jason was sitting in a chair with his pugs, watching Samuel.

"How's our guest?" Jason asked.

"She's ready for the ceremony," Samuel said. "We'll eliminate the old man after we deliver the chosen one. No one will know what happened to any of them."

"That is if no one saw you bust the windshield out of Beecham's car and then drag him out." Jason sat the pugs on the floor and walked over to the lion and raised the trap door. The pugs ran over to the trap door stretching their necks to look down the stairwell.

"You two get back before you fall in," Jason said.

Jason and Samuel disappeared down the stairwell, pulling the door shut behind them. It led to a musty room lit by torches, something that looked like a dungeon from the times of King Arthur. Carol was stretched out on a table, her arms and feet tied by iron shackles, her clothes lying on the floor nearby. Her body was covered from neck to feet by a black silk sheet. Her eyes were darting back and forth, tears running down her face.

Jason and Samuel took two black robes off a hook and slipped them on over their clothes. Jason picked up a foot-long emerald-handled dagger. He stepped up to the table beside Carol, pulled the black sheet off her naked body and raised the dagger over his head.

"We offer this mortal unto you, as a gift to your glory," Jason said.

He placed the dagger to her side and slowly shoved it into her body, all the way to the handle. Blood trickled out. He stuck his finger in the blood and marked an X on his forehead.

Samuel picked up two golden chalices sitting on the end of the table and handed one to Jason. Jason removed the dagger. Carol's eyes showed pain as blood streamed out of her body. Jason and Samuel filled the chalices with her blood and drank it.

The sound of far away drums began to pound. A smoky haze in the room got thicker and a red-horned devil appeared above Carol, stretching out his arms. The shackles fell loose from Carol and she floated up above the table to him. Jason and Samuel dropped to their knees and bowed.

A flash of lightning from out of nowhere shot into Carol's chest, pulling it apart, and she collapsed to the floor, a bloody mess.

Jason and Samuel stood and looked up just in time to see the devil holding Carol's still-beating heart in his hand before disappearing.

Samuel walked over to a flaming furnace, picked up a long hook and opened the door. The flames jumped out, trying to escape their prison of hell. He pulled a stretcher on rollers out of the furnace and placed Carol's body on the sizzling stretcher. He pushed it back into the furnace with the hook and closed the door.

They heard a banging sound from a nearby metal door. They turned toward the noise and walked over to the door with a small bar-framed window in it. Beecham's face was pressed up against the bars.

"That's enough, old man! Your time will come soon," Samuel said.

"That's what you think!" Beecham yelled out. "I called on the serpent gods to punish you and for Satan to disown you!"

"And why would the gods listen to you?" Jason said. "We'll feed you to the gutter rats. You're not even worthy of being a sacrifice."

"You will pay for your evil," Beecham said.

"It's you who will pay," Jason said.

"Let him suffer some more for his interference before we kill him," Samuel said.

Jason and Samuel removed their robes, blew out the torches and climbed the stairwell back to the house floor.

Jason sat back down and his pugs jumped up in the chair beside him and sniffed Carol's blood on his clothes.

"Soon we'll deliver the chosen one to the master, after eliminating the old man," Samuel said.

Jason nodded. "I'm going to take a shower." He got up from the chair. His pugs jumped off and followed him out of the room.

Samuel rubbed his hand across his medallion. "I may have to send Jason to you, master, he is not worthy of serving you."

Samuel heard footsteps and turned to see David Baines walking into the room.

"What are you doing here?" Samuel asked. "And how did you get in?"

"Jason gave me a key to the gate and the house to bring the chosen one here when she's ready. She called me earlier, but wouldn't tell me where she was."

"We know. Now stay out of the way."

"Why did you have to kill Brad in such a horrible way?" David asked.

"Are you questioning me?"

"No, I just don't understand."

"He had the same problems all you mortals have. Greed and lust. He was told repeatedly to leave the chosen one alone."

The doorbell chime interrupted Samuel. "Get out of my sight," he said to David and went to the front door and looked out the peephole. Detective Edward Howard was standing there, brushing snow off his coat. Samuel opened the door.

"I'm Detective Howard," the man said. "The gate was open so I came on in. Who are you?"

"I am Samuel. Mr. Steinwood's valet."

"Valet? He must be pretty rich."

"What can we do for you, Detective?" Samuel asked, holding the door open.

"You're a big one," Howard said, staring at Samuel, ignoring the question.

"Mr. Steinwood is visiting his diamond mines in Africa. How may I help you?"

"How tall are you?" Howard said, twisting his head upwards for a better look.

"Do you have a purpose for being here?"

"We had a young woman by the name of Megan Fields claim you and Mr. Steinwood were going to do nasty things to her friend, Carol West. Sounded pretty weird. You ever hear of any of them?"

"We know Megan Fields. She was going to sell antiques for Mr. Steinwood, but then changed her mind for some reason. I do not know the other woman."

"You mind if I have a look around inside? I don't have warrant, but I could say I checked everything out, make the boss happy."

Howard stepped inside before Samuel could answer.

"By all means, help yourself," Samuel said. "Just make it quick. I have a lot of things I need to do."

"I will. I've got a large pizza in the car for dinner." Howard walked into the study, stopped in the middle of the room, and looked at the painting of Joseph Steinwood.

"Who's that," Howard asked, pointing at the painting.

"Mr. Steinwood's father."

Howard nodded. "Scary looking eyes. Do you know a Father Tijeras?"

"No, why?" Samuel said.

"Miss Fields has an appointment with him to shake some kind of black magic medallion Mr. Steinwood gave her. She claims it is trying to kill her. Can't take it off, or something. And her best friend Carol West is missing."

"That's ridiculous."

"Frankly, I think she's seen one too many horror movies," Detective Howard agreed.

"Detective, if you've seen enough, I have to get back to my work."

"Yeah, I guess that's it for now. I'll come back when I have a warrant."

Samuel reached inside his shirt and grasped his medallion in his hand.

"Rise, mighty beast," he said, looking at the lion.

The lion stepped off the trap door.

"What the hell! Is that thing alive?" Howard yelled and drew his gun. The lion roared and took deliberate steps toward him. Sweat popped out on Howard's head. He shot the lion three times but it kept moving.

"Holy shit! Bullets don't faze him!"

"Nothing holy about it," Samuel said. "Now it's your time to die."

The lion jumped for Detective Howard and pulled him down, his gun sliding across the floor. The lion bit off one of Howard's arms as the detective screamed and passed out. The lion laid down by Howard and kept ripping off body parts like limbs from a dead tree. Blood ran across the floor.

Samuel rubbed the medallion and chanted under his breath in a strange tongue. The lion and Howard burst into flames and both were consumed in seconds. No trace of either one remained.

"What's going on?" Jason said as he walked in the room. His pugs ran in, smelled what happened to Howard and the lion, and ran under the couch.

"The chosen one sent a detective to find Carol West. She doesn't know we have Beecham, too."

"She'll go to the church tonight and we're done."

"She better," Samuel said. "I'll dispose of Beecham and make arrangements for us to return to the diamond mines. You get rid of David. He thinks his son didn't deserve what he got for defying the master."

"After we deliver the chosen one to the master you said I am free to do what I please."

"Perhaps once it's all done," Samuel said. "I hope your plan works…for your sake."

VIII

Beecham was sitting on the floor when he noticed light creeping through a hole in the ceiling. He must be outside the house walls then, he thought. A torture rack on the wall had come loose and was hanging down in the cell. He got up and pulled as hard as he could on the rack. It popped free from the wall. He leaned it against the wall and climbed up on it to get a better look out the small hole in the ceiling. He could see plants and flowers. Wherever he was, it was near the gardens. He climbed back down the rack, sat down on the floor again and wiped his sweaty face. He rested for a few minutes to catch his breath, picked the rack back up and repeatedly slammed it into the ceiling, making the hole bigger, dirt and rotten wood falling from the ceiling. The hole was finally big enough for him to get through…if he could gather the strength to do it.

He sat up and rubbed his chest, stuck his foot on the bottom cross piece of the rack and stepped up on the next one, stretching his arms over his head. He was short of reaching the hole in the ceiling by mere inches. He swung his arms up over his head, jumped up, extended his right arm through the hole, and hung on with his elbow as the rack fell to the floor, leaving him dangling in the air. He ran his left arm through the hole, bracing it with his elbow, and pulled himself up by scooting his elbows on the floor until he could pull his body through. He rolled over on his back, exhausted, holding his chest.

He staggered to his feet, moved across the floor to a window and looked out.

The pugs ran in, looked at the hole in the floor and sat down, twisting their heads, watching Beecham. He started looking for some kind of weapon, expecting Jason, but he didn't show up. The pugs continued to watch.

He saw a ladder propped up on a fence surrounding the mansion, next to a tree the landscapers had been trimming. He looked at the pugs, unlocked the window, climbed out and staggered across the lawn to the ladder. He climbed up over the wall, wheezing with every breath, and fell into bushes on the other side. He forced himself to his feet; his eyes watering, clothes torn, with cuts and bruises on his face and hands.

He stumbled out into the street, cars dodging him from both directions, waving his arms frantically for someone to stop.

Samuel had heard the commotion and was standing on the ladder, looking over the wall. He reached inside his shirt for the medallion as a police car came into view, slowing down to a stop beside Beecham.

Just then, Beecham collapsed.

Samuel dropped the medallion from his hand and climbed back down the ladder.

Beecham looked up at a police officer approaching him, too weak to get up on his own.

"I need help. They're trying to kill me."

"Who's trying to kill you?" the tall, thin officer asked.

Beecham was having trouble catching his breath. He raised an arm and pointed to the mansion.

"They murdered a woman in there," he finally said.

The policeman looked at where he was pointing.

"That's Steinwood Mansion, a pretty famous place," the officer said. "What's your name, old man?"

"William Beecham. I'm a professor at the university. Jason Steinwood and a witch doctor kidnapped me."

Just then, another police car pulled up. Sergeant Wells stepped out and approached the scene.

"What you got here, Henry?"

"Not sure, Sergeant. He said someone was murdered up at the Steinwood place. And then something about being kidnapped…by a witch doctor? Thinks he's a college professor. Keeps holding his chest. I think he's drunk, or on something."

"You better play it safe and get him to a hospital," Sergeant Wells said.

"There's one nearby, I'll take him there myself."

Beecham was stretched out on a bed in the emergency room, two nurses hooking him up to a heart monitor, inserting an IV and taking his blood pressure.

He woke up and grabbed one of the nurses by the arm. "I have to get a message to someone."

"You're going to be okay. We'll do that later," one of the nurses said.

"It's not about me. It's life or death for someone else. Call Megan Fields for me. Tell her to go to the church as planed. The number is…" He passed out after telling the nurse the number.

A doctor walked in and started examining Beecham, looking at the heart monitor.

The nurse handed Doctor Nolan his chart and a piece of paper on which she had written down what Beecham had said.

"He's going straight to heart surgery, get him

prepped," Doctor Nolan said. "I'll make the call for him after his surgery." He stuck the paper in his pocket. The nurses unhooked Beecham, lifted the bars up on the sides of his bed and wheeled him out.

Hours later, Doctor Nolan opened the double doors to the surgery room dressed in scrubs splattered with blood and walked over to the nurses' station. He took the paper from his pocket and dialed the phone number. Megan answered.

"This is Doctor Nolan at St. Mary's Hospital. I just performed heart surgery on a William Beecham. He made it through, but will be out for a while."

"What happened?" Megan asked.

"He had a heart attack is all I know. Police brought him to the emergency room. He gave me your phone number and said to—" the doctor looked down at the note again, "—to tell you to go to the priest. Hope that makes sense."

"It does," she said. "How is he?"

"I think he's going to recover. It was close, though. Had to do a triple bypass."

"Thanks, doctor. Tell him I'll go to the priest."

"Uh…okay, I will," Nolan said and hung up. He looked at a nurse assisting him. "Strange call," he said and went back to treating Beecham.

IX

Megan drove to San Gabriel Cathedral in the suburbs. Sitting in her car across the street from the church, she watched people come out the massive front doors. The church bells rang and a priest stood on the first step against a handrail, saying goodbye to everyone coming out. She assumed it was Father Tijeras.

She got out and walked across the street once the departing parishioners slowed down to a trickle. She found the priest inside.

He saw her, nodded and walked up to her.

"Megan Fields?"

"Yes. Professor Beecham sent me. Father Tijeras?"

"Yes. I understand you're wearing a chakra medallion? Dangerous. The devil will take you, body and soul."

"That's why I'm here," Megan said. "The professor said you could save me."

"Not me. The almighty will take care of that. Where is Professor Beecham?"

"He's in the hospital. He had a heart attack."

"I'm sorry to hear that. We had many good times together in Africa."

"That's what I heard," Megan said. "And about this?"

"The chakra has been sent to conscript your soul through the lust of the flesh and make you a willing mate of the devil," Father Tijeras said.

"Get this thing off me then!"

"You are a foolish person. You should have never worn it."

"I was tricked."

"I will present your problem to the almighty and ask that you be liberated from the spirits of evil. After that, it becomes a battle of the gods to decide your fate."

"What about the god you serve?"

"Excuse me for a moment. Stay where you are. I'll tell the sisters to not let anyone disturb us. We have to prepare a ceremony to remove your soul from the devil's quest."

Father Tijeras left Megan and walked into his sanctuary office. He pulled out his phone and dialed.

"She's here," he said. He put the phone back in his robe and walked out into the assembly area.

"Do you have a cell phone with you?"

"Yes," Megan said.

"May I have it, please?" he asked her. "We can't allow any interruptions."

Megan hesitated, then handed him the phone.

"Come with me," he said.

They walked down a hall to a door. He opened it and switched on a light hanging over stairs to the basement. The light left a dark spot on the opposite side of the room. He ushered Megan through the door and closed it.

"We have to go down there?" Megan asked.

"That's where you will become the bride of the devil."

"Oh no." Megan turned to run, but suddenly Jason appeared and was standing between her and the door.

"Your friend Carol was sacrificed," Jason said. "And that's what will happen to you, too, if you don't cooperate."

"You son of a bitch," Megan said.

Samuel stepped out of the dark at the foot of the stairs.

Jason and Father Tijeras grabbed Megan by the arms and dragged her down the stairs. Samuel moved to her, reached out and picked her up with his huge hands. She was kicking and screaming as he carried her to a long table in front of an altar. He placed her on her back, tied her with ropes, hand and feet, to the table in a spread-eagle position. He then ripped all her clothes off with a sacrificial dagger and covered her with a black silk sheet.

"Juan, bring the consecrated oil and light the altar candles. She must be re-baptized," Jason said.

Father Tijeras went to a nearby cabinet, took out a gold lamp and walked back over to Megan. He removed the sheet and poured oil all over her body, then put the black sheet back over her, sat the lamp at the end of the table and lit the candles on the altar.

"You have been re-baptized in the name of Satan," Father Tijeras said. "Your name has been entered into the Book of Evil. You are now ready to join the master for all of eternity."

She twisted and turned, fighting the ropes. "You hypocritical bastard!"

"I believed once," Tijeras said. "No more. Your god failed me when I asked him to save my village from volcanic devastation. I then became a follower of Satan, the real god. You should feel honored."

Samuel and Jason put on their ceremonial robes and joined Tijeras at the table.

"It won't be long now," Jason said. "He will be here soon."

A hooded figure wearing a red robe appeared from the dark. He pushed the hood back from his head and stepped out into the candlelight. It was Gary Roberts in his flight uniform.

"No not you too," Megan said.

"Happy?" a deep, echoing voice said. But it wasn't Gary's voice. "I took this form to please you. I can be him when we copulate, if you want."

"Oh my god," Megan said, breaking into a sobbing rain of tears.

"Not god. Me. I sent your fly boy to hell. You belong to me now."

A second later, Gary's image was gone and had been replaced by Megan's mother.

"What about this one?" A roar of laughter spilled out from his booming voice across the room.

Megan screamed, groaned and struggled at the ropes. Suddenly, one of them snapped, and she squeezed her hand out of the rope and jerked the sheet off her. It floated down over the altar, catching on fire from the candles.

Father Tijeras rushed to the table to extinguish the flames devouring the sheet. He knocked the lamp off the table, spilling oil on his robe. Flames leapt to his robe from the sheet, igniting the oil. He spun around, trying to get out of the burning robe, throwing a piece of it into the curtains. Flames shot up from the curtains to the wall.

The devil changed his appearance again, becoming a horned, red beast, snorting from his oversized nostrils, his fiery eyes flashing. A bolt of lightning shot across the basement, striking him and knocking his body against a burning wall.

"You're doing this now," he said, looking up at the cross above the door at the top of the stairs, "but I'll have the last laugh."

Megan clawed frantically at the ropes as the walls began to burn. Father Tijeras was lit up like a torch on the basement floor.

Samuel rushed toward her. She rolled off the table on the opposite side and ran for the stairs.

Jason and Samuel pulled their robes off and gave chase up the stairs. She scrambled up to the door but it was locked. Jason and Samuel were only steps behind.

She was trapped.

Suddenly, the door opened. A nun was standing there, staring at her naked body.

"I saw smoke coming out from under the door," the nun said. "Where are your clothes, child?"

"You did it again," the devil said. "My turn." He waved his hand and the nun burst into flames, falling to the floor, burning.

Megan darted out into the assembly area. A woman stopped praying, mesmerized by a naked body in a church. Megan jerked the coat off the woman's back and put it on as she ran outside through the snow in the street. Her Mustang was gone. She saw a taxi sign on an incoming car and walked out in the middle of the street, holding her arms up in a 'stop' position like a traffic cop.

The taxi stopped. She ran through the slush on her bare feet and jumped in the taxi.

The man behind the wheel was staring at her.

"Go! Go! Go!" she said.

"You're crazy, lady," the driver said.

Megan was looking out the back glass for Jason and Samuel. "Go, damn it," she said, never turning her head and rubbing snow off her feet.

"Where to?"

"Anywhere, just get me the hell out of here."

He shook his head, pressed the accelerator, and spun off through the snow.

Jason and Samuel walked out on the street and looked it up and down.

"She will go to the old man now," Jason said. "I'll go get her."

Father Tijeras walked up to them. At least, it looked like Father Tijeras. They knew it wasn't really him.

"Samuel, you have always been one of my favorite demons until now. You fail me again and I will send you and your mortal to hell forever. I want a son with the mortal touch to show what I can do to the gods. If I have to get her myself you're of no value to me anymore."

"I will deliver her," Samuel said.

In the blink of an eye, the devil was gone.

X

"Saint Mary's Hospital," Megan said, glancing back out the back window.

"Cost you twenty dollars. You got the fare?"

Megan stuck her hand in the stolen coat. A small purse was in the pocket. She opened it and found a twenty dollar bill, two credit cards and a driver's license.

"I'll be damned," she said. "Maybe someone is helping me."

"What was that?"

Megan looked at his picture and name. "I've got it, Abdul." She waved the twenty at him. "Haul ass."

Abdul pressed the accelerator, made a U-turn, and headed for the hospital. As they drove by the church again, Megan scooted down in the seat and could see Jason and Samuel were gone.

A big neon sign was glowing in front of the hospital as Abdul drove in and stopped in front of the rotating doors.

"Here," Megan said, handing Abdul the purse with one hand and the twenty with the other. "Get this purse back to the lady on the license." She tugged the coat tight around her and walked into the hospital through the rotating doors.

The only people in the lobby were a man sitting on a couch behind a newspaper, and a young female volunteer at an information desk.

"Can I help you?" the young lady asked.

"Yes, please. What room is William Beecham in?"

The volunteer ran her finger down a paper. "Room 544." She saw Megan's bare feet and stopped her as she walked to the elevator.

"Miss," she said. "You can't go up there bare-footed."

Megan didn't answer. The elevator door opened, Megan got on and the door closed behind her.

The man reading the newspaper dropped it on a table and stood up. It was Jason.

When the elevator door opened on the fifth floor, two security guards were standing there, waiting for Megan.

"Miss, you have to have shoes on in the hospital," a short, stocky security guard said.

"Find me some," Megan said and kept walking down the hall, looking for Room 544.

"You'll have to leave," he said.

"I'm not leaving. I have a friend here I need to see now." She turned another corner in the hallway and two more security guards were waiting for her.

They grabbed her by the arms and the coat fell off. The two security guards let go of her like she was on fire.

"You're naked," one said.

"I wasn't, until you jerked my coat off," Megan said.

"What we do now?" one of the security guards said, staring at Megan.

She picked up the coat and put it back on. "Get out of my way."

"You have to come with us," the stocky one said. "You don't have shoes and you're not properly dressed." They grabbed her arms again and escorted her to the elevator.

Jason was standing behind a stairwell, listening. After they put Megan on the elevator, he walked out into the empty hallway, slipped his hand into his pocket and took out a long switchblade knife. He snapped it open, looked at the number 544 on the door, and went inside.

Beecham was hooked up to an IV, heart monitor and blood pressure machine, fast asleep. Tubes were sticking out the side of his gown.

Jason shoved a chair under the door handle, twirled the switchblade in his hand and walked up to the bed.

"You're the cause of all my troubles."

He raised his knife and the door made a loud squeak. He stopped and looked at the door. The chair slid back from the door a ways and a nurse stuck her head in.

"What's going on in here?" She pushed on the door until the chair slid further back. The opening was big enough now for her to walk through.

Jason raised his knife again. Beecham's eyes popped open. He rolled off the bed to the floor on the opposite side as Jason's knife came down hard on the bed, barely missing his target. The heart monitor fell against Jason and the nurse pushed her way in.

Jason charged the nurse with his knife, grabbed her by the hair, pulled her head back and carved a jagged red rope around her neck. Blood gushed out, coloring the front of her white uniform a bright red in seconds. He let go of her hair and she crumbled to the floor.

The room door came open again and a man in blue scrubs walked in, holding a syringe.

"What the hell?" he said when he saw Jason with the knife. He dropped the syringe as Jason pushed past him and ran out into the hallway, towards the stairwell.

The orderly ran out behind Jason and saw him opening the door to the stairs.

He busted the emergency glass and pulled the lever, the hospital alarms began going off. He ran to the nurses' station down the hall.

"A nurse and patient have been attacked in Room 544," he said to the head nurse. "The man who did it ran down the stairs. Get some help to the room, I'll call 911."

The security guards were escorting Megan through the lobby when the alarms started blasting everywhere in the hospital.

"What's happening," the young lady at the information desk asked a guard holding on to Megan with one hand and a phone to his ear with the other.

"There's been an attack on a nurse and the patient in Room 544," he said to the other security guards.

"That's Beecham!" Megan jerked loose from the guards and ran to the stairs.

"What do we do about her," one guard said.

"Let her go," another one yelled. "We've got to cover the doors and do our job."

Megan took two steps at a time to the fifth floor, slammed the stair door open and ran to Room 544.

Doctor Nolan was in the room on his knees, examining the blood-covered nurse, and then picked up a bed sheet and draped it over her body.

"She's dead," he said.

Beecham was lying on the floor, conscious and looking around. Megan ran over to him, sat down beside him on the floor and grabbed his hand.

"You're alive," Beecham said. "Thank god."

Megan looked up and read the name tag on the other man's white coat: Richard Nolan, M.D.

"Let's get him back in bed," Nolan said. Two orderlies came to assist. They carried him to the bed and hooked him back up to the IV and the other machines.

"Who are you," Nolan said, looking at Megan as he placed the stethoscope to Beecham's chest.

"Megan Fields."

"I spoke to you this morning. Did you see the priest?"

"Yes, unfortunately…Didn't turn out so good."

"Too bad." Nolan continued examining Beecham.

Nurses were running in and out of the room with medical supplies when a man with a wrinkled brow, days-old beard stubble, wearing a cheap blue suit and an overcoat walked in, gazing around the room with his steely gray eyes. He took off his coat and pitched it onto a chair, showing a police badge and a pistol on his belt.

"You in charge of this, doc?"

Doctor Nolan looked at the badge on the man's belt. "Nothing to be in charge of," Nolan said. "Just taking care of patients."

"Got a call there was a stabbing here. I'm Detective Sizemore."

"Yes, a nurse is dead," Nolan said. "That's my heart patient on the bed. He was attacked, too, but didn't get stabbed. And the young lady standing by his bed with no shoes on is a friend of his."

"Can I speak to him?" Sizemore asked.

"He's out right now but maybe later," Nolan said.

Sizemore walked over to Megan, gave her a once-over and looked at her bare feet.

"I'm Detective Sizemore, miss. The doctor said

the patient is a friend of yours. He have any family?"

"No family, just me." Megan glanced at Sizemore then her eyes went back to Beecham.

"What kind of a relationship do you two have?"

"None of your business."

"Do you know you don't have shoes on," Sizemore said and grinned.

"We'll, I'll be damned. Where did they go," Megan said, exaggerating a shocked look but never looking at Sizemore.

"Would you happen to know why someone tried to kill your friend?"

She turned to Sizemore and looked him up and down.

"Yes. It was Jason Steinwood and his giant Samuel. They're demons. They were going to breed me to the devil. I reported my best friend missing and what was going on with me to the police, but haven't heard anything. You better go get him. He'll come after me and the professor again."

Sizemore looked at the doctor and they grinned at each other.

"Did you see Steinwood here?" Sizemore asked.

"No, but it's him," Megan said.

"Miss Fields, Jason Steinwood is one of the most upstanding citizens we have in this city. He's always donating to charity and giving money for special causes."

"That's all a front for what he really is."

"Hmmm…well, now I've heard everything."

"I'm not crazy."

"If the shoe fits," Sizemore said, and looked down at Megan's bare feet.

Megan pulled the coat tight around her and walked over to the doctor.

"Doctor Nolan, will you tell the professor I'll be back soon. I have to get some clothes and shoes." She headed for the door.

"Wait," Sizemore began, "I have more questions."

"I just told you who's responsible," Megan said. "Being a lady, I won't tell you where you can place those shoes you keep suggesting."

Megan rushed out into the hall, Sizemore following. "I'll see you later," he yelled as she walked down the hall. Sizemore stopped and waited until she got to the elevator, shook his head and walked back into the room.

"Do you know her?" Sizemore asked the doctor.

"No," Nolan said and looked at the tape from the EKG he was running on Beecham.

Sizemore looked down at the professor. He was taking deep breaths in his oxygen mask.

"He doesn't look too good, doc."

"That's why I'm here."

"That lady's strange," Sizemore continued. "I'll have to look her up. Let me know when I can talk to your patient if he comes around. He may be the one that put her up to accusing Jason Steinwood. If so, she may need more than shoes."

XI

Back at her apartment, Megan closed the balcony drapes and went to the bedroom. She dropped the coat, took the medallion off and laid it on the bed. Severe pain shot through her body. She was beginning to have second thoughts about submitting to the devil, just to ease the pain. She picked up the medallion and hung it back around her neck and the pain subsided. She didn't want to stay in the apartment any longer so she skipped a bath and hurried to dress, putting on high top shoes to wear in the snow.

She looked in the bedroom mirror again. Her image was coming and going like she was stepping away from the mirror. But she wasn't. She hadn't moved at all. The changing reflections were making her dizzy. The room started whirling around and around, faster and faster. She fell to the floor and passed out.

A green mist began spilling out of the medallion, first filling the room and then settling underneath Megan like a soft blanket. She was lifted onto her bed. An instant later, she was floating through the sky, wearing a flowing white gown made of white fluffy clouds, zooming over mountains and jungles beneath her as she soared through the air.

She came to a village below her and was whisked through darkness to a palm leaf bed in a straw hut. The green mist settled over her, bringing a dim soft light above. Megan tried to move, but couldn't.

A tall man appeared at the foot of the palm bed. His shaved head was shining like glazed chocolate. His body beaded with sweat and covered in tattoos from head to toe. Ostrich plumage formed a headband and leopard skin decorated his lower torso. Bone bracelets covered his upper arms. Another man appeared, smaller in stature, but a replica of the first. They walked up on each side of the bed, turned to face Megan, locked her arms down and tied her legs to posts.

A third man appeared naked. He was the one from her dreams. A golden-tanned Adonis. The men on each side of her took a tighter grip.

The third man reached down, took hold of Megan's gown and ripped it from her body. Drums began to beat. He knelt down beside the bed, rubbed her body gently from head to foot, then leaned over the bed, kissing her passionately, and rose to his feet. He smiled, then turned and walked away, disappearing into the mist.

The two men let go of her and, without warning, she woke up in her bedroom on her own bed.

She sat up and looked around the room. No one else was there. She felt her body. She had her clothes on. The medallion still hung around her neck. She slid off the bed and looked in the mirror, her image still coming and going. She grabbed a bottle of Vodka and poured a full glass before drinking it down like water. She poured another glass and drank it, too. The glass fell out of her hand. She staggered back and fell across the bed. She coughed, grabbed her stomach and threw up on the bed, vomit covering her face.

She got up, wobbled to the bathroom, wiped her mouth with a towel and looked in the mirror. She wasn't there. She yanked a drawer open, took out a hand mirror and looked at it. Her refection was there for a moment but then was suddenly gone. She looked back in the bathroom mirror. Only her clothes and the medallion were there. She collapsed on the floor, dropping the hand mirror on the tile floor and busting it into a thousand pieces. She leaned back against the bathtub in a daze and stretched her legs out across the floor. She saw a piece of the hand mirror looking back at her. She picked up the jagged piece and looked at her face. It was there and then it wasn't.

She screamed. "You're never going to have me!"

She dug the mirror glass deep into her wrist. Blood flowed out across the floor like a small river.

A heavy, smoky haze began to twirl in the shower. Something moved inside the haze and a human form appeared. It was a woman. She was wearing a white robe from neck to feet. She looked at Megan, reached down and placed her hand on Megan's bleeding wrist. The blood stopped like it was turned off by a faucet. Megan looked up through blurry eyes. It was Carol.

"I was just thinking about you," Megan said. "I would have called you if I had a phone. Where have you been?"

"Dead," Carol said bluntly. "And so are you. You just bled to death. That's why I'm here."

"No I'm not. I'm just drunk," Megan said.

Carol took Megan's arm and stood her up. "You see yourself in the mirror?"

"No."

"Because you're dead. I'm dead. We can be seen by the naked eye but we have been taken away from human form in mirrors."

"How can that be?"

"Jason and Samuel sacrificed me to the devil. They took my life but not my soul. The same thing happened to you by cutting your wrist. You took a shortcut to your soul," Carol said and grinned. "I made a joke."

"What's so funny about being dead?"

"It's not, but we're going to a better place."

"Maybe all this is a dream?" Megan said.

"It's not. I came to take you to Sunny Land. To a new life, where the gods will protect you from evil for all eternity. It's the place you want to be. The highest celestial plane in the universe, and all that. I don't know how I made it there. Must be because I know you."

"Sunny Land?" Megan asked. "The highest celestial plane in the universe is called Sunny Land?"

"I didn't name it! I just came to tell you about it."

"But…you can't really be here if you're dead."

"Try me."

Megan reached out and touched Carol's face.

"You're really here," Megan said. "You're not dead."

"You're hard to convince. Can a living person do this," Carol said and disappeared before Megan's eyes, then reappeared on the other side of the room.

"No. I believe you now."

"We have to destroy Samuel before we can go to Sunny Land."

"And if we don't?"

"We're up shit creek," Carol said. "He will take us to hell. We can't do it with mortal weapons, either, but that thing hanging around your neck can, when it makes contact with Samuel's medallion. The medallions are high-voltage banks that attack each other for control. They will fry Samuel like a bug zapper if he has both on him at the same time. The trick is, you have to keep yours on and drop it around Samuel's neck to make contact with his. The spell will be broken and Samuel will be nothing more than a bad memory."

"How do you know that?" Megan asked.

"Trust me."

"You were always there for me when I was alive," Megan said. "I guess I'll just have to trust you now that I'm dead."

"You sure as hell do, or we'll both be kissing the devil's ass."

"Don't you get in trouble for cussing?" Megan said.

Carol looked at Megan, studying her for a moment in disbelief. "No wonder the devil wants you. You're too damn perfect."

"Same ol' Carol," Megan said.

XII

Jason and Samuel were in the study, the pugs sitting under a nearby chair. Jason stood up and moved under his father's painting. The dogs followed him.

Samuel was standing on the greasy spot that was once Detective Howard and the stuffed lion.

"You have failed again," Samuel said. "I raised you to serve the master and the demons of hell, but you never took it seriously. Failure means death. The master has deserted you and now I must, as well. You no longer have my protection."

The medallion hanging around Samuel's neck

was vibrating.

"I have always taken my loyalty serious," Jason said. "I'll get the girl. I promise."

"It's too late for you."

Samuel lifted the medallion from around his neck. Jason ran for the door but it was locked. The pugs ran under the couch and peeked out at Jason and Samuel.

"Please," Jason pleaded. "Give me another chance. I'm like your son."

"There are no families in hell." Samuel lifted his arms and waved his hand across Jason's face. Fire shot from the medallion to Jason's eyes, turning them a solid black, leaving him blind. His left eye popped out of his head and rolled across the floor. He fell to his knees, screaming in agony.

"You couldn't see the truth," Samuel said.

Samuel raised his hand over Jason and the evil green mist poured out of the medallion, covering Jason's entire body. He burst into flames and burned, until the only thing left was a small puddle of liquid and a single eyeball beside it. The pugs came out from under the couch and sat down on each side of Jason's remains.

Samuel turned away and walked by the painting of Joseph Steinwood.

"I'm tired of looking at you, too," Samuel said. "Now I have to finish what your son couldn't. Wasted my time all these years." He walked out of the room and the painting began to burn.

Megan and Carol were standing in the kitchen where they could see the front door and the balcony, waiting for Samuel.

The doorbell rang and the front door flew open. Megan's next door neighbor Tom was standing in the doorway with a blank look on his face, blood trickling out of his mouth, his arms dangling at his side.

He fell forward and crashed to the floor. David Baines was standing behind him with a big smile on his face, holding the ceremonial dagger in his hand, blood dripping from it. He stepped over Tom's body into the room, looking at Megan.

"You can't escape," he said.

"You too?" Megan asked.

"I picked you out for the devil myself," David said. "I'm Samuel's right-hand man now. He had to eliminate Jason for failure. You will be kissing the devil with passion by the time we get through with you."

"You bastard! Why did you have to kill Tom?"

"I hate nosy neighbors, don't you?"

"You little cockroach," Carol said. "Oh, Sunny Land, hear my plea – make this little man as small as he can be."

The dagger fell out of David's hand as he shrunk to the size of a cockroach and ran across the room, under a chair.

Carol picked up the chair and dropped it behind

her. David ran toward the balcony doors. She stomped her foot on him, leaving nothing but slimy particles behind on the floor.

"That was a horrible thing to do," Megan said.

"If we don't defeat Samuel, that may be what he does to us," Carol reminded her.

The wind blew hard against the balcony doors and knocked them open, throwing the drapes inside. Snow blew into the kitchen and a raven landed on the railing and screamed. The lights went out and the silhouette of a huge figure could be seen on the balcony by the light of a full moon.

The raven was gone. It was Samuel now.

He stepped through the blowing snow into the room, dressed again in leopard skin, plumage blowing back and forth on his head, tattooed serpents snarling on his arms, and the medallion glowing bright. He was holding the crooked stick in his hand.

"I will take your souls now," he said.

"I don't think so," Carol said. "I know what a big pile of shit you are. I just smashed David. He won't be any help to you."

"He never was. All mortals are failures like you."

Samuel placed his hand on the medallion and pointed the stick toward Carol. A stream of fire shot across the room. She disappeared before it could get to her. It hit the wall and set it on fire.

"Where are you, Carol?" Megan screamed.

"The whore has abandoned you again," Samuel said.

Silver dust whirled in front of Megan as Carol

reappeared. "Never," she said.

Samuel raised his stick and stepped closer to Megan.

"Now!" Carol yelled.

Megan grabbed her medallion and leapt toward Samuel like a basketball player trying to make a game-winning shot. She flung her medallion around Samuel's neck, the striking tattoo snakes just missing her. The medallion slid down on Samuel's neck and made contact with his. Flashes of fire shot from both medallions, striking each other, and spun Samuel around so quickly he didn't have a chance to grab them. Fire ropes bound his arms against his body, his tattoos pinned against his arms. He dropped the stick and it started to burn. The medallions continued to clash. The binding fire ropes were slicing pieces of his body off like a well-oiled chainsaw through an oak tree, until nothing was left but a pile of pukey, slimy, smoking meat in the blowing snow.

"We have to go now," Carol said.

"Can I see the professor before we go? I want him to know what happened."

"Sure," Carol said. "And what about your dad?"

"I don't want him to know yet. He won't understand me telling him I'm dead. It's different with the professor."

"You have a point," Carol said. "Let's go."

The cold snow was blowing the steaming pile of Samuel's hot glob of body meat, making the air smell like a skunk barbecue.

XIII

Carol and Megan materialized in Beecham's hospital room.

Megan walked over to Beecham's bed. He was asleep. She gently shook his arm. He woke up and rubbed his eyes to make sure he was seeing Megan, and then took her hand.

"I was worried about you, child," he said and smiled.

"I was too," Megan said.

"You must have seen Father Tijeras," he said.

"I did, but it was a mistake. He was one of the devil's disciples. But he's dead now. I am, too."

"What! You don't look it," Beecham said and looked at his other visitor. "This must be Carol."

"Yes," Megan said. "She's also dead."

"We don't have time to tell him the whole story, Megan," Carol said. "She is going with me to Sunny Land, professor, to save our souls. We're running out of time here."

"I wanted you to know what happened," Megan said. "Father Tijeras was burned alive. Samuel killed Jason and we destroyed Samuel by clashing the medallions together."

"That's quite a story," Beecham said. "I knew when I saw Carol with you. I was in a cell in Steinwood's dungeon, listening, when they murdered Carol. I was supposed to be next, but escaped."

"I did a stupid thing," Carol said. "I called Jason and chewed him out for giving Megan the medallion. He traced me to my apartment."

"You will soon be in a place even the devil can't get to," Beecham said. "I read much and learned even more from the mystics of Tibet. Sunny Land is the highest plane of the universe."

"See, he's heard of it," Carol whispered to Megan before turning toward Beecham. "I'll see you there someday, professor."

"I hope so."

"Oh, I almost forgot," Carol said. "Megan, I thought you might want this. Close your eyes and hold out your hands."

"What is it?"

"Just do it."

Megan did and felt something soft in her hands. She opened her eyes. She was holding Midnight. He looked up at her and she wrapped her arms around him.

"So you know, cats don't have nine lives," Carol said. "By the way, sorry about Gary."

"I feel terrible about what happened to him."

"You didn't do it. The devil always finds someone to blame for his deeds."

Suddenly, a bright light flashed in the room and went away as quickly as it had come.

"Time's up, Megan," Carol said.

She stepped up to Beecham's bed and handed him a small, glowing heart-shaped jade jewel.

"Never let this get far from you. You can call on us by placing it against your heart and saying our names."

Beecham nodded and closed his hand around the jewel. "I understand."

Megan and Carol hugged his neck and stepped away from the bed, Megan still holding her cat.

A swirling, sparkling light appeared in the room, shining brighter and brighter and spinning Megan and Carol around and, suddenly, they were dressed in shimmering white robes.

"Goodbye, professor," Megan said.

"I'll see you again," he said.

Megan drew Midnight close to her and they were gone with the light, leaving Beecham alone.

Two puffs of thick, black smoke came under the door in Beecham's room and hung in the air for a moment before settling on the floor, drawing Beecham's attention.

Small feet with claws extended from the smoke, followed by little, flat black faces. Jason's two pugs had materialized on the floor before Beecham's eyes. The pugs licked their noses and looked up at him.

Beecham grabbed his chest, placed the jewel against his heart and squeezed.

"Oh my god…Megan, Carol, come get me before it's too late," he said, rubbing the jewel against his heart. He picked up the call button with his other hand and started pressing it frantically, his eyes never leaving the pugs.

A streak of swirling white light shot through the ceiling then exploded across the room like fireworks, throwing large, blurry shadows on the wall.

The light lifted Beecham off his bed, wrapped him in a cocoon of radiance, and evaporated into nothingness like he had never been there.

The light and Beecham gone forever.

The room dark as midnight.

THE END

ABOUT THE AUTHOR

John L. Lansdale was born and raised in east Texas. He is married to the love of his life Mary. They have four children. He is a retired Army reserve psychological operations officer and a combat veteran that served three tours in Vietnam with numerous medals and awards. He is a graduate of a Texas police academy and a state certified peace officer. He is an inventor, country music songwriter, performer and television programmer. He produced the television special "Ladies of Country Music" and several other programs. He goes back to the Sun Record days and was introduced to Elvis Presley by Mary on their first date when Elvis was a seventeen-year-old student at Humes High School in Memphis and a ticket-taker at Loew's State Theater.

John has produced a variety of albums and music videos for country artists in Nashville along with songs for movies, with one as recently as 2018 titled "Tremble" for an upcoming film. He has hosted his own radio shows and won awards for radio and television commercials. He was a writer and editor for a business newspaper. He has worked as a comic book writer for Tales from the Crypt, IDW, Grave Tales, Cemetery Dance and many more. He co-authored Shadows West and Hell's Bounty with his brother Joe. He is the author of Slow Bullet, the four-part Mecana detective series, Long Walk Home, Zombie Gold and several others.

John's novel Slow Bullet was reviewed by Publishers Weekly as a must read page-turner with constant action and compared his work to that of popular 1950s author Mickey Spillane. The novel Long Walk Home was a finalist in the fiction category for the National Indie Excellence Awards. The novel Zombie Gold received great reviews including a Booklist review that praised it as a superb story with characters that came alive. Kissing the Devil received praise a pulp novella. All titles are still in print with new ones on the way.

John was recently inducted into the Gladewater Museum.
His motto is: Never Give Up.

THE MECANA SERIES by JOHN L. LANSDALE

HORSE OF A DIFFERENT COLOR – Book #1

Dallas PD Detective Thomas Mecana is on the hunt for a serial killer terrorizing the Lone Star State. Joining him is Darcie Connors, a young officer working her first murder case. With hard work, and some luck, they soon discover a most-unusual serial killer case with murder in its very genes.

WHEN THE NIGHT BIRD SINGS – Book #2

Detectives Thomas Mecana and Darcie Connors are on the trail of a new suspect. With an ever-growing suspect list, Mecana must toe the line between friend and foe. Each action leaves them sitting in the crosshairs of danger. One wrong move could mean the end.

TWISTED JUSTICE – Book #3

Dallas Homicide Detective Sunday Verves is looking into the suspicious deaths of local drug runners when she discovers a potential suspect who hits too close to home. When the trail leads her south of the border, she enlists some old friends to track down the suspects.

THE BOX – Book #4

Detective Thomas Mecana and the gang get back together for another case. Mecana soon finds the new case involves old evidence. This horror-filled novel brings the series full-circle to where it all began.

OTHER TITLES from JOHN L. LANSDALE

SLOW BULLET

Army veteran Clark McKay is searching for the truth behind his best friend's murder. This search takes him across the globe, where he meets a multitude of characters and is forced to wade through the murky Washington DC waters of corruption. Clark McKay wants to find a murderer... but what happens when he uncovers so much more?

LONG WALK HOME

The O'Rourke family lives on a fading farm in the small town of Angel Point, Mississippi. With family, friends and neighbors fighting overseas in WWII - and rising racial tensions back home - the summer of 1944 turns into a nightmare of murder and loss. Trenton O'Rourke reflects on those days and how his life was forever changed.

THE LAST GOOD DAY

As the Civil War draws to a close, Major Rance Allison is wounded in one of its last battles. He later awakens in an enemy field hospital only to find out he is now on the same side as those he was fighting. The war is over. Missing a limb, his home and his family, Rance sets out to find a new life for himself.

BROKEN MOON

Left for dead, Billie Jo will stop for nothing on her search for vengeance.

OTHER TITLES from JOHN L. LANSDALE

BEYOND IMAGINATION

An all-new short story collection spanning a variety of genres. Also contains the fan favorites:

BOY AND HOG / BOY AND HOG RETURN

In the deep woods, anything can happen. A group of white-collar workers with a hand-drawn map trek into the wilderness for a hunting expedition. But out there, will they be the hunters or the prey?

EMERGENCY CHRISTMAS

Join the Albright family and the guest who surprises them just in time for the holiday. Along the way, they discover sometimes crisis brings a family closer together.

OTHER TERRIFIC TITLES from BOOKVOICE

John L. Lansdale
-The Last Good Day (Hardcover - eBook)
-Long Walk Home (Hardcover - Paperback - eBook)
-Beyond Imagination (Hardcover - Paperback - eBook)
-Kissing the Devil (Hardcover - Paperback - eBook)
-Slow Bullet (Hardcover - Paperback - eBook)
-Horse of a Different Color (Hardcover - Paperback - eBook)
-When the Night Bird Sings (Paperback - eBook)
-Twisted Justice (Paperback - eBook)
-The Box (Paperback - eBook)
-Zombie Gold (Paperback - eBook)
-Emergency Christmas (Chapbook - eBook)

Joe R. Lansdale
-The Magic Wagon (Ltd. Edition Hardcover – Paperback - eBook)
-Bubba Ho-Tep & Bubba and the Cosmic Blood-Suckers Double-Feature (Paperback)
-The Complete Drive In: A B-Movie Triple Feature [Includes Books I, II, III] (Paperback - eBook)
-The Drive-In I: A B-Movie with Blood and Popcorn, Made in Texas (eBook)
-The Drive-In II: Not Just One of Them Sequels (eBook)
-The Drive-In III: The Bus Tour (eBook)

John L. Lansdale and Joe R. Lansdale
-Hell's Bounty (Paperback - eBook)